For Jeff and the velociraptor. Very ferocious.
—A.M.R.

For Mr. McCarthy
—Z.O.

Text copyright © 2017 by Anica Mrose Rissi
Illustrations copyright © 2017 by Zachariah OHora

First Edition, June 2017
10 9 8 7 6 5 4 3 2 1
FAC-029191-17083

Printed in Malaysia

This book is set in Caslon / Adobe
Designed by Phil Caminiti
The illustrations were created using acrylic and pencil on BFK Rives printmaking paper.

Library of Congress Cataloging-in-Publication Data

Names: Rissi, Anica Mrose. | OHora, Zachariah, illustrator.
Title: The teacher's pet / by Anica Mrose Rissi ; pictures by Zachariah OHora.
Description: First edition. | Los Angeles ; New York : Disney-HYPERION, 2017.
  | Summary: When a class pet proves to be more than a handful, the students agree they cannot
  keep him, but how will they convince their teacher, Mr. Stricter, who loves the strange creature?
Identifiers: LCCN 2015019173| ISBN 9781484743645 | ISBN 1484743644
Subjects: | CYAC: Pets—Fiction. | Schools—Fiction. | Teachers—Fiction. |
  Humorous stories.
Classification: LCC PZ7.R5265 Te 2017 | DDC [E]—dc23
LC record available at http://lccn.loc.gov/2015019173

Reinforced binding

Visit www.DisneyBooks.com

The TEACHER'S PET

Written by **ANICA MROSE RISSI**

Illustrated by **ZACHARIAH OHORA**

Disney • HYPERION

Los Angeles   New York

On the day the science project hatched,
our whole class was amazed.
We'd never seen Mr. Stricter so excited.
"I always wanted a pet," he said.

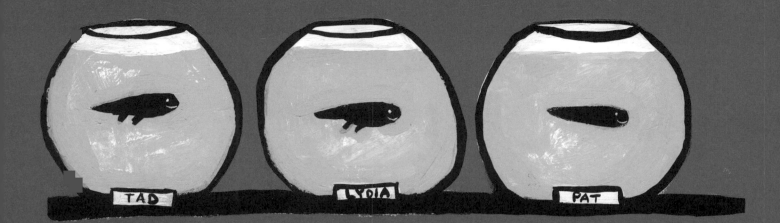

Our tadpoles grew and grew.

Soon it was time to release them into the wild.

But Mr. Stricter said we could keep just one.

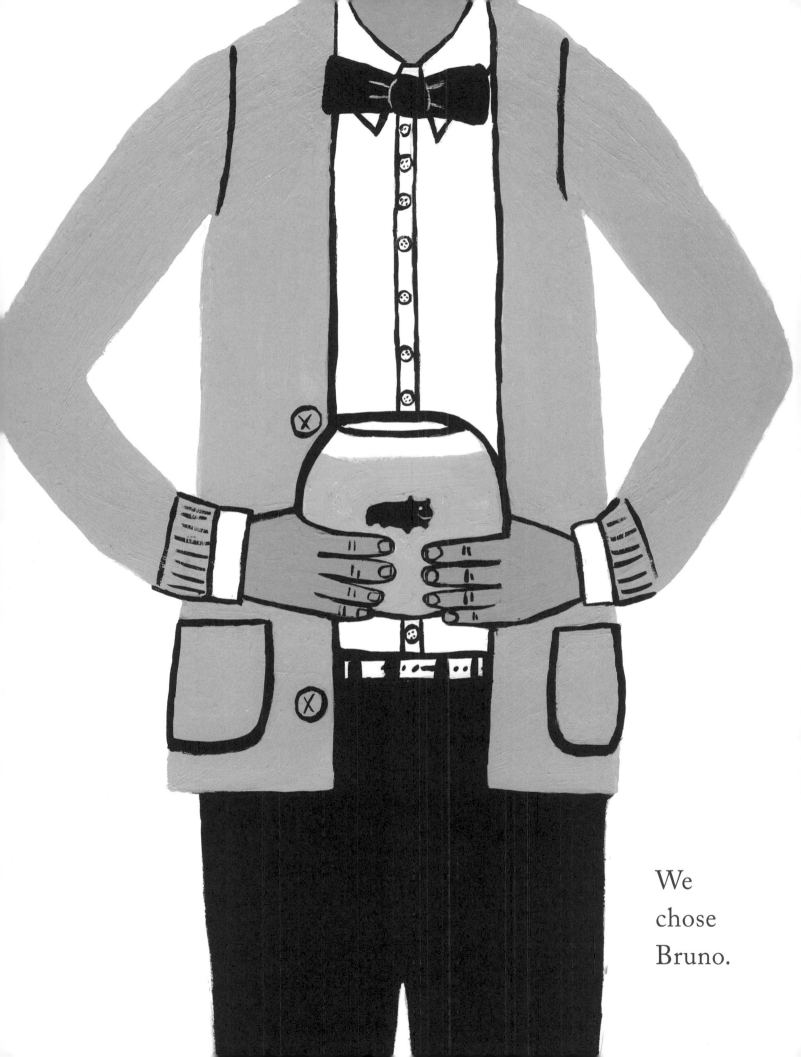

We
chose
Bruno.

Bruno had been the last frog to hatch,
and he was the smallest.

We brought in bugs and worms to feed him.

But he preferred eating our markers.
And our scissors. And our books.

"Look how he's growing!"
Mr. Stricter said.

Our teacher was right. Bruno grew and grew.
And grew.
And grew.

Everyone could see that
Bruno was trouble.
Everyone except Mr. Stricter.

CRUNCH!
MUNCH!

"He's very energetic," our teacher said.
"Just like a pet should be!"

RWAARRRRR!

"See? He loves to play."

"But Mr. Stricter," we said, "he's—"

"Look how clever he is!"

We held a class meeting at recess.
Everyone agreed: Bruno had to go.
He'd grown and grown into a
bigger and bigger problem.
We just couldn't keep him.

But how would we convince Mr. Stricter?

We tried to tell him.

"Bruno snores during silent reading."

"He farts for show-and-tell."

"He hogs the swings."

"He eats our homework!"

But Mr. Stricter wouldn't listen.

"You're overreacting,"
our teacher said.
"Bruno wouldn't
hurt a—"

Before Mr. Stricter could finish,
Bruno had swallowed him whole.

"Give him back!" we demanded. "Give him back, now!"
But Bruno wouldn't listen.

We begged. We shouted.
We made threats. We tried bribes.
But Bruno's stubbornness grew and grew.
We had to get our teacher out of there.
But how?

"I know—the plant!"

"The plant!" we agreed.

We held it under Bruno's nose.
His sniffles grew and grew.

And grew.

ACHOO

Mr. Stricter flew out like a snot rocket.

He shook Bruno's slime from his ears.
"Good news," he said.
"I found the missing homework."

"It's time to release Bruno into the wild," we said.
"He's not meant to live in a classroom."

We'd never seen
Mr. Stricter so sad.

We walked Bruno to the frog pond and said goodbye.

Mr. Stricter squeezed Bruno in a giant hug.
"You were a wonderful pet," he said. "But I think you'll be happier out here where you belong." Bruno blinked four times, unfurled his tongue, and gave our teacher's face a lick.

Then he jumped into the pond with a **SPLASH.**

"Maybe he'll come back to visit," we said.

Mr. Stricter's smile grew and grew.

The next day, our new science project hatched.
Soon it was time to release the butterflies into the wild.

Mr. Stricter said, "Maybe this one would make a good pet...."
But we had an even better idea.

We helped him choose the perfect one.